CW00516543

MISTRESS CARTOGRAPHER OF THE UN-LIGHT

MISTRESS CARTOGRAPHER OF THE UN-LIGHT

Robert Czerniawski Rocherry

CZERNIAWSKI ROCHERRY
DARTFORD   KENT

For Pauline Hazel Cheesmur.

ISBN 978-1-9996985-0-8
Printed in Great Britain by
Arthur H. Stockwell Ltd
Torrs Park   Ilfracombe
Devon EX34 8BA

20th July 1969

Until 20:18 <u>UTC</u>

She was abducted in Poznań.

She arrived there on Saturday to take part in a meeting which she needed very much in this difficult moment of her translator's career. She decided to cover that considerably long distance from Krakow's suburbs to Poznań by driving her beloved car.

It wasn't a caprice of somebody who is terribly fond of driving (who she was as a matter of fact) or one who loves to be seen in her own car which is so rare in this homogenised gloomy country (who she wasn't).

It was a knowledgeable decision of somebody who had paid for this knowledge traveling numerously by PKP-trains and suffering their awful standards and who once said *Never again*.

She decided that because a trip like this done with PKP- Polish Railway in 1960s would appear even more exhausting than almost 500 kilometres driving on poor-quality roads.

So, she set her arrival and booked a hotel room in Bazar-

hotel on Saturday despite two planned meetings being arranged for both Sunday (the informal one) and for Monday (the formal when a manuscript was supposed to be handed to her).

At nearly forty years old a woman needs to rest properly after such long driving to look fresh the next morning. Safona wasn't one of those women who make a career utilising their femininity, but in the current circumstances she needed to mobilise every available trump card in her deck.

The arrangement of the coming meeting was rather peculiar, nevertheless she was to some extent desperate to turn a blind eye on this peculiarity.

She wasn't afraid of life in poverty.

Although Abel, her husband, had retired from the army a few months ago following the forced resignation of his commander and closest family friend general Rozłubirski[1], still his pension was high enough for them both and their daughter. Their son was already independent.

---

[1] General Edwin Rozłubirski (1926-1999) must be considered as an extremely unique figure despite his military career in the inglorious communist resistance and subsequently in the armed forces of communist Poland.

What symbolically encapsulates his entire life: he was the only one among the communist resistance officers who was decorated with the Virtuti Militari cross for his merits and gallantry in Warsaw Uprising by general Tadeusz Bor-Komorowski the commander of the Home Army (the resistance organisation reporting to Polish Government in London)

https://pl.wikipedia.org/wiki/Edwin_Roz%C5%82ubirski

Abel had turned a devastated old cottage on the outskirts of Krakow into a modern comfortable house. There was no practical reason to be afraid of joblessness, but it wouldn't be consoling for Safo.

A little while ago she was one of the most esteemed and best paid translators in the country. One year ago, everything was turned to rubble due to the anti-Jewish campaign initiated by the communist party.

However not by the campaign itself though Safona was a Jew, indeed.

The campaign was deliberately designed to look as if it was a grass-root-movement, to avoid a resemblance e.g. of Stalin's purges executed by his secret police.

It doesn't mean that the Polish secret police were entirely passive in the campaign of 1968, but in most cases their activity was reduced to "benevolent leaks" about somebody's genealogy. Often even such "help" was redundant because the party's campaign had awakened the darkest particles of numerous people's souls. Also happening were grotesque situations when some Jewish (and not only) were denouncing themselves as Jews on purpose to obtain a one-way-passport and in this way escape from behind of the Iron Curtain. For instance, one of them was Safona's twin brother.

But such scenarios do not refer to the collapse of Safo's

career. At first, she took her husband's surname, which wasn't a Polish one, but definitely by any measures wouldn't be recognised as Jewish.

The name Safona Chardan de Rieul couldn't be associated with Jewishness...

So called "benevolent leaks" also don't apply to her case because of official- and even more because the unofficial connection of lieutenant colonel Abelard (Abel) Chardan de Rieul.

Actually, the collapse of Safo's career wouldn't have been possible without the anti-Jewish campaign 1968, at all, but it couldn't happen without another component which was her too-outright expression.

Employing a pragmatic point of view, one would say that she organised the collapse of own career by herself. Furthermore, if she weren't the wife of such a persona as Abel it would have ended far worse.

After the long year of adversities she was almost inclined to this opinion.

Therefore now, Safo was determined, almost desperate to rebuild her professional position. Therefore, peculiarities in the meeting's arrangement weren't able to discourage her. Peculiarity in this business in this country has usually only one explanation – *Some well-connected moron had already got a commission and now needs a skilful brain to fulfil the taken commitment... and he/she is ready to sacrifice some fraction of the expected emolument.*

Probably her husband would have considered those peculiarities as alarming irregularities if he knew anything about them, but he didn't. The recent period of their espousal wasn't the best one, so they weren't sharing many details in talks. Sometimes it is good to ask a professional even if we perceive him as irritating.

Safo was desperate enough to take the risk of being humiliated by some well-connected-whoever while it did not cross her mind what kind of menace truly awaited her in Poznań.

She has been abducted from Poznań cuffed and blinded and dropped on a lorry's floor.

Initially she hadn't any idea what was happening, let alone about details of her surroundings due to chloroform, which was used in the very moment of abduction. Nevertheless the trip wasn't a short one, so she has had plenty of time to restore consciousness and to deduct several details of her situation.

It wasn't the first horrifying event of her life. She was not always the prosperous professional living much above an average material standard of sovietised Poland. And it wasn't the first time when a horror was brought to her life by Russians.

Safona Lilienthall was originally born in 1930 amid a highly educated prosperous cosmopolitan family, but then she was re-born as a new person in a dark and for most of this time cold hideout. Over three years of Safo's late childhood had been spent mostly in secret rooms constructed by her father in the decommissioned workshop of his friend.

Especially, the ordeal of three autumns and three winters had trained her instincts for life without sight, in primeval darkness, because a use of any light was a menace of an imminent uncover. Such an exposure meant for a Jewish kid almost certain death. This experience trained her to see surroundings through blindness of total darkness and not only this.

Safona had been restoring her peacetime's nature for long years after WW2, but now this other wartime -Safona commenced her awakening.

There came the moment when the forgotten part of her nature started paying its tribute.

Now she was able to assess the size and kind of vehicle and also the approximate number of wardens according just to physical sensations alone. Her body's inertia confronted with the vehicle's dynamics was providing her with knowledge about the distance between soldiers' boots. *The vehicle's floor is too vast for a van, while lack of some characteristic swoosh neither draught of air indicates the type of its superstructure.* Additionally, as a military-officer's wife she was quite familiar with types which should be taken into consideration. *This one must be a sort of mobile field-command post. Such vehicles aren't really fast, and its engine doesn't work to its last limits, thus if my sense of time works properly I can figure out the covered distance... I believe my unconsciousness lasted less than a quarter, so we must be now some 100 kilometres from Poznań. Are we heading to one of the big Russian military bases in Polish Pomerania?.. Or in the opposite direction... to USSR? Any other destination makes much less sense... I think.*

The almost perfect lack of chats between wardens was very telling in respect to the question *Who/what they are?* or even to some extent *What is their job about?* This almost perfect discipline of silence maintained for at least 2 hours wasn't normal among Russian uniformed and even clandestine personnel.

Her husband Abel's, former career as a top-officials' bodyguard and then as Warsaw Pact's senior military officer acquainted her with all Russian servicemen' "species". *None of them was able to maintain such long-lasting silence except under extremely unique circumstances. Only top-servicemen acting accordingly to very special and precise orders are able to keep their mouths shut. Maybe I was wrong in recognising them as Russians during the meeting in the Malta Regatta Course?... No, I was right... They are as Russian as hell... only with very, very, very special orders.*

The lorry stopped ultimately after a few final

manoeuvres. Four very strong men dragged Safo out of it. She tried to wrestle mostly for testing their strength and number. These four carrying her were strong. They were more than strong enough to execute their orders regardless of any defiance even if she were a fit man. So, Safo turned her attention on the sounds of her environs.

Nothing beyond birds' calls and footsteps. Then a door squeaked and the footstep's sound changed, but not only that. There was another accompanying one. This was like the rattle of machinery.

They were heading towards the source of the rattling and Safona, even quite literally, due to the fact that she was being carried with her head forward. The rattling was coming nearer and nearer and suddenly went off after a subsequent door's terrible noise being an unique and ghostly combination of multiple squeals and squawks. The carrying men cornered to the right and the footsteps switched to a new tune. It was parquet.

Finally Safona had been laid on some rough fabric, something like a standard military blanket and another door was shut just near her head... rather a grille than door, actually. She was listening to men's footsteps walking away for a couple more seconds and at last the door's squeal-squawk marked that she was left alone for some time. *Who knows how long it is to be?*

Left alone, Safona started striving to find any idea of what she could do in such circumstances?

Doing a query through her own adulthood experience and expertise she didn't come up with anything useful. Whereas the older stash of semi-instinctive instruments which just started awakening during the trip from Poznań, commanded her to cry. It wasn't a cry of powerless despair.

– Ani yiv-at lecha ba beitsim. – She yelled out a sentence in Hebrew even before her mind realised any rational purpose of such action.

No matter what she yelled out, neither is there anybody out there to listen, nor one who would understand the sentence. Most probably no one within this vicinity would.

What did matter, was her voice proliferation. This is the stuff primordially obvious for bats, though not only for them. Now, she knew that the room was quite big... *some twenty by twenty meters and over six meters high.*

In her distant past she had spent hundreds, maybe thousands of hours training a visualisation of spaces which couldn't- or shouldn't be seen and what is happening within them.

She still hasn't got any concept of the potential actions which should be undertaken, but wasn't distressed by this absence. Her mind was being possessed now by a parade of images and feelings memorised over the mid-1940s.

De facto orphaned non identical twins were hiding for three years in decommissioned workshop supported only by the mother in law of their parents' friend and her grandchildren... *only trustworthy people on entire planet... Madam Katarzyna and her grandchildren... especially the oldest, Gustaw, who was killed shortly before the so called "liberation".*

She was eleven when her mother was arrested and sent no-body-knows-where by Russians, then a few weeks later Germans came to Lwów and perhaps they arrested her father who was looking for some trace of his wife.

Now, she felt, that all this old art of surviving had fervently returned as if the "liberation" of Lwów happened just twenty-five days- not twenty-five years ago.

Still cuffed and blinded Safona tried to stand up. Making this effort she bumped her own head into a metal bar, so then she very cautiously examined the space around.

– I am in a cage – She said aloud and sat down.

A few minutes later the creepy squeal-squawk-noise was launched by the ghostly door like an arrow into her ears and mind. *This one marks somebody's arrival... only one person... most likely a male but not one of those musclemen who brought me here.*

The sound of steps hashed nigh of the cage. An overcharged silence encompassed the surroundings. Safo held her breath but nothing happened for an unbelievably long 15 seconds then suddenly "a visitor" caught her forearm through the cage's bars, uncuffed her and almost in the same moment he tore the canvas sack from off her head. She arose slowly without looking at "a visitor". Finally she turned her eyes to him.

He is staring at me like a black-marketeer at a stolen car.

He was staring at her while Safo rather tried to scan the surroundings of the circus cage in a possibly discreet way.

"A visitor" was a slim guy of approximately her age and height.

He was unusually resembling one of the Russian propaganda posters' types. The one who is always junior-leader, young officer, engineer or scientist in some cutting-edge-domain of science. This resemblance made this horrible situation a bit tragi-farcical. Whereas his outfit only amplified her sense of the tragifarce. He was dressed in some hybrid of tropical suit and military uniform as if he just popped in from taking a break in the production of some pretentious film.

Sometimes a fear manifests itself by an hysterical amusement. Not in her case however ... not yet.

The only thing making him less-farcical was a Czechoslovakian fully-automatic pistol geared in a non-Russian or cinematic way. *As long as I am able to discern such contrasts, for that long I am in control of my fear.*

Eventually "a visitor" began to talk. He was speaking

Polish diligently hiding his Russian accent in what sounded like a dialect of north-eastern Polish provincials. *Well, maybe he is just a Pole from soviet Belarus?... Does it matter?* – the linguistic part of Safo's mind still acted as if she wasn't in this woeful situation.

– I am sorry that I cannot introduce myself, but my real identity is classified whereas there is no point in giving you any fake name. Please undress ... naked ... and throw your clothes outside the cage, please.

– А пошел вон[1] – Safona bursted out offensively in Russian.

...Fuck your thuggish courtesy. Do you want to buy me by speaking Polish? My Russian is much better than your Polish. – she added in her mind.

The men did a step back and took her on gunpoint. He wasn't polite anymore, but was still talking in Polish.

– Undress...now... or...

– Зачем тогда мне раздеваться, как ты хочешь меня убить? Мне боле удобна умереть одетом.[2]

Suddenly Safona noticed a glimpse of perplexity in the facial expression of "a visitor". This glimpse made her to realise that her sentence was rather equivocal; that it was bringing an unintentional undertone. *Damn! What am I*

---

[1] Get the fuck out.
[2] What for then I should undress myself as you want to kill me? I prefer to die being dressed.

saying?! It could be interpreted almost as a wink done by a prostitute. The realisation sent an acute impulse of anxiety/dismay through her body and mind, but a very few seconds later a powerful sobering waive retained her thoughts. It overcame everything and made her even stronger. She started analysing in half-instinctive contingency mode.

It does not matter at all.

He is testing me.

He has had enough occasions and resources to strip me without this thuggish courtesy; without speaking Polish and the ostentatious gun-pointing.

In these circumstances the only one thing making all these things coherently reasonable is the test's scenario.

If the test's scenario consists of a rape amid other elements, then I will be raped and there is nothing that I can do to prevent it... Analogically, if there isn't such an element, I can do very little or nothing to provoke such an "improvement" of their scenario.

When Safo was just stating her conclusion inside her own mind, "a visitor" decided to cease the impasse. He made a dozen of steps heading towards the gymnasium's entrance. The creepy squeal-squawk-noise echoed once again all around the room. Then he shouted sharply some indiscernible commands down the corridor.

Instantly six people marched into the gymnasium.

Five of them were tall musclemen dressed identically

as their commander whereas the sixth was different; similar height, but much more slender and subtle despite a mismatched jumpsuit and balaclava which she was wearing.

Yes... She... Undoubtedly, the sixth is a woman... And what is really sinister, she is of my height and most likely of my body-structure too... They have their own me-ish... It cannot be a good sign of any kind.

One of the musclemen pushed a big old-fashioned key into the lock and turned it. Another caught resolutely both Safo's arms and pulled her out of the cage as if she was a fox which was about to be skinned. Safona exercised determined defiance just to manifest her human dignity but a disproportion in strength was resembling the fox vs. skinner confrontation. Suddenly amid the scuffle Safona spotted the masked woman approaching with a wet rag in her palm, and then... everything disappeared in a cloud of chloroform.

The smell of chloroform was telling her with a few second's notice that she is to lose consciousness; If she was able to think normally in this very moment she would anticipate a loss of her clothing; But neither she nor anyone was able to predict one lucky and immensely game-changing gain heralded by this nasty smell.... A button... a very common button in quite an uncommon place.

The Button of Luck

Her consciousness commenced restoring itself. The pitch-black started fading. After some half a minute the sluggish17 metamorphosis of a gloomy darkness entered its diluting stage and Safo spotted two women's silhouettes sitting behind a café-garden-table like those of the Malta Regatta Course.

Did I collapse waiting for the meeting? Did I just undergo a nightmare about this entire Russian stuff?

Whatever abnormality was running her mind before this moment, it didn't stop, apparently. It transmuted to be even worse; definitely weird. She comprehended the worsening through a realisation that she knows both of these women and at least one of them cannot be here by any means. The black-haired woman was beyond any doubts Aurora Lilienthal; her mother. The second one seemed to be familiar, though in an uncanny way. The second woman looked a bit like a bleached version of her mother; as if the Asian blackness of the mother's hair, eyebrows and lashes was just replaced by the almost-albino Nordic blond. Her appearance resurrected one more track of Safona's memories from 1940s; the extremely ghostly- though paradoxically advantageous one. Safo's mind went adrift into an archaeology of her bleared memories related to the second woman.

I did meet or at least see her, firmly, but when?... When I saw her?.. Before WW2? ... Before my mom's disappearance?... Or after that?... Before daddy's disappearance, or ?...

Her mother's benign voice terminated Safo's still fruitless excavations.

– My Ferret-pup, take a seat with us, please. – The Aurora's voice sounded unchanged; it was exactly the same as it was in 1941.

– Mom, it has been 30 years since we talked last time... at least when we talked outside my dreams... Your voice cannot sound identically... Mom, you even look like in springtime of 1941...

– Have you noticed that?... All the better. To be entirely precise, you are seeing me as I looked in December 1948...– The latter date unexpectedly opened one more of the forgotten vaults within Safo's memory regarding "the Nordic woman-companion". The revelation was so arresting that Safona sensed a compulsion to verbalise it in her mind.

"The Nordic woman-companion" started visiting my ... dreams... my dream-like catatonic moments just after the abduction of my mom... of my Ori... and she ceased to

appear in the end of 1948... yeah, the 1949 was the first year without her... It cannot be an accident... there is a bond between the two, but what kind of bond... The single thing I would be sure of now is that: I have never met "the Nordic woman-companion" in the real world.

Aurora or Ori as she had been called by beloved people seemed to be waiting until her daughter organised her thoughts and was able again to concentrate. Eventually Aurora reinstated her utterance. Her words were apparently referring to Safona's just completed thoughts as if she heard them.

– ...so, my Ferret-pup, you know that we are not the components of your space-time-continuum, very well... by the same means, you are just losing your certainty, whether, you still are a part of it (?)... Well, you are, firmly... this is the simple part.

Also, you are not sure, whether you have retained any influence on the development of events in your life(?)

The answer is YES... especially with our little help.

Alas, it doesn't mean that I can save your future by a snap-shot of my fingers, but you have always been my Magic Ferret-pup, so we can accomplish numerous things working together.

The Ferret-pup phrase has found its way into the deepest deposits of Safona's mind only as it was used by her mother for the third time.

Only this third time reclaimed the original charge of this loving nick-name which had been given to her back in the forgotten past of her childhood. Only now, Safona figured out how meticulously she had erased this nick-name, or even the act of erasing itself. This realisation of seemingly secondary importance prompted a shock-wave of undefined anger within her mind; the anger without any defined cause or a defined malefactor. This shock-wave made her open eyes... literally.

The picture before Safona's eyes was the same as this before the last sedation done by the Russians. Directly before her eyes was the grill of the circus cage and behind it still was the same old Prussian-style gymnasium, almost unchanged since the Keiser Wilhelm II's times; only the political watchwords written in Cyrillic and new parquet were marking all the changes of the last 50 or more years.

In front of her eyes nothing had changed, but within the cage changes were quite considerable... Safona wasn't alone anymore within it. Two women sat next to her; Aurora and her "Nordic companion". Safona once again pushed herself to organise her thoughts into rational frames, but her mother again was faster vocalising the answer for the not-yet-formulated question.

– You are perfectly correct my Ferret-pup, this is something different... this what you see... this is not a post-anaesthetic hallucination... in the margin, it is regrettable that you didn't choose medical studies!... back to the essence... by some means we are physically here.... and I hope you will embrace this issue soon. However in terms of your world' physics, we are somewhere else at the moment.

Safona took a breath like one who is to say something eternally crucial, but she froze at this stage still not being able to formulate anything that should be said; anything that she by herself would recognise as such. Aurora was waiting.

Finally she vented out by an almost irrelevant postulate.

– Call me by my real name.

– OK. You too, please... and by the way, her name is Ragna... And stop sitting here completely naked because this cage is really taken from a real circus, so heavens knows what microbes are here... dress yourself ... they left a jumpsuit... it is awful but at least properly disinfected.

It is time to discuss really important issues. The machinery-rattling, you had heard in the corridor is being made by a big German industrial freezer. There are two corpses inside; a woman who resembles you by height and a few overall features was a Georgian student making some extra-money from prostitution; a man inside the freezer used to be a German tradesman; his greed and unhappy marriage with his parents in law business led him into the hands of the GRU... The company of his father in law installs such freezers... He had believed, gullibly, that the GRU gave him some "courier's job"... a commission which would free him from being blackmailed... You know a few ГРУщиков[1] and their institution... there is no-way to get rid of them even if one made only one single insignificant "business" with them... And now, he ended as мороженное мясо[2].

The Russians' plan assumes that the frozen couple "will die" in the car of the German guy, somewhere between this place and the East-German's border. His Mercedes had been specially converted by GRU-people to get on fire... inextinguishable fire after any impact... of course after the "special installation" is armed.

Accordingly to the plan of this operation, you must survive... unfortunately, only according to the plan "A". Even this optimistic version wouldn't be in fact called the fortunate-one. It assumes that they will be keeping you as a hostage to the end of your days, most likely... as they were keeping me until 1948, though for different reasons. Your chances to ever meet any of your beloved people in this scenario are nearly zero.

The "A" scenario cannot move on if your death-certificate is validated by recognition of "your" alleged corpse... which actually is already being frozen in this corridor. You are supposed to be "stored alive" as leverage on your

---

[1] GRU-people
[2] The frozen meat.

husband and possibly somebody else. Thus, there must happen an identification of burned corpses after the orchestrated road accident, but it "should fail". Perhaps in the mortuary your husband will be approached by someone before his statement regarding the corpse would be put on the official record... so, maybe they would even organise an ultra-quick meeting for you two to amplify his desire of a next one... the longer one.

I don't have to say what is to happen if Abel will refuse, or if he will start tinkering something...

– No, Ori... you don't have to...I know. But this alternative simplifies itself effectively... because if they show me to him after such "an enactment" then I would give you a guaranty that he will be tinkering with this situation to the last blood's drop retained in his veins... Not necessarily because he loves me that much, but because Russians had destroyed his world once and he would rather prefer to die then allow them such a repetition... so I am already dead.

– Yeah... the Russians failed in profiling him... They recognised him as a pragmatic, stoic or even opportunist, whereas your Abelard is a camouflaged dormant zealot... but....

– Yes he is the forth kind of WMD[1] and almost nobody knows that... You are describing Abel as if you were living with him?

___
[1] **W**eapon of **M**ass **D**estruction

– To an extent … I was… I was observing you, so him as well…

– How long?

– Since 1949.

– Without saying a word?

– I was obliged not to interfere

– In different circumstances I would stop talking with you for a year… at least.

Safona realised that she is slightly adopting herself into dialoguing with her own dead mother, so her rationality responded by a counter-attack.

*Why such an organically rational person as I am, cannot get away from this hallucination?… Ba, I don't even feel a willingness to do this… Despite the fact that it cannot be anything else but the hallucination… She said: "…**by some means we are physically here…. However in terms of your world-physics, we are somewhere else at the moment.**" I am not a physicist, but I am rather capable of discerning, what belongs to the physics, as opposed to what belongs to psychiatry, and wouldn't qualify her statement as material for psychiatry… "She said!" this is almost funny!… yet, it must be my own split mind, but from where has it gained such trans-dimensional concepts?… Had I translated some scientific or science-fiction's texts, over these last years before I was blown out of this business?*

Still, hallucination is the only one thing, which any sane mind would accept.

Then, why have I this unwavering sense that it is not hallucination?

Maybe because my subconscious is just telling me, that lunacy is the only one tactic left in my disposal(?)

Yeah... Russians checkmated me... this is the truth... so my brain (recently exposed for two sedations within a short period of time) is producing mirages as a sort of a self-defence(?)... Yeah, my instinctive reality assessment was telling me the same even earlier... I am checkmated!... checkmated on the several chessboards at the same time... ouch.

Let's analyse what would happen if I followed the lunacy tactic... An insane woman is most likely unmanageable for GRU-people... except an occasion if they needed a suicide-bomber, but there is no point to organise so complicated an action to obtain the suicide-bomber in Poland, or any country behind the iron curtain... thus the insane-woman will become the no-longer-useful-woman, so.... she must turn to be the death-woman.

As only this clown in fake uniform will qualify me as the insane-woman, he will kill me... Apparently we are still in some initial stage of their operation and on such a stage any damage is cheap, so he will kill me and... no woman, no cry.

Thus, if the lunacy tactic possesses any usefulness then it isn't the right moment to employ it yet… I have to consolidate my strengths and get rid of my mom and her Nordic friend… Ragna.

"Get rid!" …Easy to say. When Safona turned her sight to the side where the two women were sitting before, she saw them again. Furthermore, Aurora started her utterance exactly from the point where she paused a few minutes ago.

– … So, if Abel will start tinkering anything, then the Russians will switch to plan "B".

They prefer to avoid this because it complicates the so called legalisation of their agent, but they are fully prepared for this scenario too.

We cannot accept the plan "B" because this assumes that you will be killed as the first and then Abel as well as your children… and not only… The GRU wants to implant their agent initially in Israel with a further option for USA.

– …Orf?… – Safona pronounced her twin-brother's name as if she was sighing with anxiety. Her memory instantly revitalised the other angry feeling from last year when Orfeusz/Orf stated in a phone call that "he is starting a new job in Israel and since next week any direct contact with him will be impossible".

He told me breezily, that I would have to contact him through some murky office… he dared to tell me something like that after all these things we went through together... he even suggested that it would be more manageable if I emigrated to Israel... I was so infuriated, that I would slap him in his face if it wasn't a phone call. I had forgiven him a few minutes later, so after that I wasn't trying to comprehend, what such "indirect contact" is for(?)... I understood this only now.

– Yes. This is my son who interests the Russians more than anything ... at least on the current stage. This fact implies an additional role for your husband... To keep you alive, they expect him to persuade your brother to a collaboration. If your husband failed, then they are to apply another plan "A-minus". This one differs from the plan "A" in...

–... In killing Orf instead of me and my family in Poland?... Am I right?

– Yes you are... It isn't a good option for the GRU because they see Orfeusz as a sort of springboard for their agent, or agents, but his potential refusal would compromise the entire channel, so...

– Then, what can I do now? Should I start enabling the ideas of these Russians to keep my beloved people alive?

– No... Because even if you and all your relatives could collaborate with the GRU in an exemplary way, there still remains a danger of the unpredictable changes within the Russian scenario on their side... for instance, some new boss can scrap the operation overnight... we have no idea when such a hypothetical new factor would happen, but... we can be quite sure that a termination of their operation due to any reason must result in the termination of your life and lives of your family... my family too... by the same means, actually.

Hence, You must escape.

– My escape is equal with the death of them all...

– On the contrary... This is the only way to save them... of course only if you escape today ... within the coming hours... There is only one inconvenience... this escape must be like the death... forever and ever.

– Should I shred this blanket and make a halter for myself?

– No, It isn't an option which I would offer for my own child... It must be like death, but not the death.

– Then what?

– Look here, Safo... Do you see the brown button in the gap between the door frame and the lock?

Safona turned her attention on the lock. There was the button torn away from somebody's uniform, indeed.

– This is a slam lock... The lock didn't work properly because of the stacked button ... just push... – For the first time Ragna took her part in the conversation. Safona executed Ragna's command and moved out of the cage.

– What now? She asked looking at Ragna.

– Kacapy[1] are already heading the scene of "the accident"… only the GRU-woman has left here… She is our key to get out of here and a passport to the free world… It isn't an easy part due to her strength, training and experience… I think she isn't a virgin in killing people… such an expertise changes a lot…

– And she is some 10 years younger than you… – Aurora threw in the additional observation.

Then Ragna was continuing instructions:

– Climb up on the cage's top… From that place you can lift yourself on the beam over the cage… Then go along the beam to that window …over there… and try to memorise the terrain around the gymnasium.

Safona got to the window after she executed all Ragna's commands.

She saw most of the Russian facility which apparently used to be once a Prussian boarding school or so; the area was very small like one for military standards countered by a red ribbon of brick-wall fitted with barbed wire. There were streets and regular town houses just a few hundred meters behind the wall.

She saw her mini parked by the side of the building and an opened gate being guarded only by a movable barrier and two bored soldiers melting under the July's sun, and … nobody else…

---

[1] Derogatory call for Russians.

Not so long time ago Safona and Abel's conversations were still being long, frequent and concerning a vast variety of issues. A fact that some topic was interesting for one of them was enough to make it interesting for the other; sometimes more, sometimes less but still interesting enough to memorise automatically some details. This is why Abelard exceeded his fellow-officers in intellectual culture, while some times Safo was able to avoid consultancies with experts while working on some text's translation.

Safona's mind was just unpacking boxes stored in her memory one by one.

One of such conversations was about the Russian military presence in Poland.

Over the 1945-1957 period Russians had had an absolutely free hand in establishing and dealing with their military facilities all over Polish territory.

There was an opulent number of them.

Among so called "the objects" were huge ones as well as tiny little; there were those of clearly military purpose as well as others being factually agrarian-ones or completely undefined-ones.

Poland was being treated as a one additional Russian *gubernia*[1] or an occupied country.

---

[1] An administrational entity in generals similar to the English notion of county.

The sluggish process of changes started under the 1957 Gomułka-Khrushchev-agreement. On this day 20 July 1969, the application of this agreement was still uncompleted after twelve years of processing.

Small facilities like this one were being scrapped first. As this particular one is still functioning it means this must have a special purpose, or it has been "conveniently forgotten" by the Russian Ministry of Defence.

After 20:18 <u>UTC</u>. Still 20 of July 1969

The door's squeal-squawk suddenly crumbled the silence of the gymnasium when Safo was just moving back along the long horizontal beam; more specifically, when she was just "hugging" a vertical element of the roof structure.

The GRU-woman entered the room. Her entire presence was manifesting an unnatural aggravation/nervousness.

Safo got petrified on the horizontal beam embracing with her all strength the vertical one. Her pulse was striking from within as if an animal implanted into her body were trying to extricate itself frantically.

The GRU-woman stood still in front of the opened cage apparently having no idea that her prisoner was just over her head now.

Apparently she was staring at Aurora who was just sitting in the opened door of the cage.

How is it possible?

It seemed that a dumbfoundedness of the Russian is to fossilise the entire room. Finally she yelled hysterically.

– Кто ты, блядь?[1]

There wouldn't be any doubts as to whom she was directing these foul words... she is speaking to my Ori... but how it is possible? If she sees the figure from my hallucinations, then that means I am not hallucinating ... at least not about my mother... rather about all this story, instead(?)... No... it is impossible to hallucinate such a detailed story... The only explanation is that I am unconscious and getting through one of those anaesthetic nightmares, which allegedly happen sometimes.

Meanwhile Aurora rose slowly and said very politely.

– Меня зовут[2] Aurora Rudolfowna Lilienthal... А вы? Как вас звать, девочка [3]?

– Ты откуда здесь, сука тупая?[4]

The GRU woman took her pistol from the pocket screeching her last words and pointed it at Aurora.

This picture stripped Safona of her all rationalisations. What has remained, was the pure instinct. Instinct alone drove all subsequent actions before she even sensed, what she was doing.

She was hanging on the beam's edge for a fraction of a second above the GRU-woman; then she released her

---

[1] Who the fuck are you
[2] My name is...
[3] How should I call you, my girl?
[4] How did you get here you stupid bitch?

grip and fell on the woman beneath so skilfully as if she had been trained along side her husband's subordinate paratroopers. Her feet struck the neck and head of the Russian and almost instantly slipped down along the body while Safona's hands involuntarily clenched around the neck of the GRU-woman. Eventually the impact pushed the Russian off her balance and she fell forwards with Safo holding her from behind. Her body bumped into the parquet and something cracked loudly inside her. The bone-cracking-noise was echoing over the room for a few seconds; nobody moved.

After these seconds Safona realised that she is actually siting on a human being in agony, so she elevated and moved a few steps back nervously.

Meanwhile, Aurora approached the retching body with the military blanket in her hands.

– My Ferret-pup, take a seat please... make some space for a physician at work...

Aurora wrapped the head of the Russian in the blanket and tightened it. She was holding the blanket stretched in this way for almost 2 minutes, until the GRU-woman ceased her retching. Now she turned to her daughter again simultaneously searching for a pulse in the Russian body– ... Are you distressed due to this, my Ferret-pup?... They would do the same with her, or left her crippled to the end of her days ... you are perfectly aware how excruciating is the fate of disabled people in the Soviet

Union... aren't you... OK, the time of decease 20:20 UCT.

– Actually, mom, I don't feel distress or anything similar... I know maybe four soviet citizens who I care about... more or less... Definitely I don't care about their secret personnel... they stole my life together with the Germans several times, then they tried once again in early 1946 when Abel rescued me and my brother... They were behind almost everything damaging for my entire life... No...

I am just staggered by... Look, when she took you at the gun point I started believing that you must be some sort of projection... something like a scientific-ghost, whereas it appeared you are strong enough to suffocate a human... more-or-less...

– Your scientific intuition works very well... Really, you should have taken a different subject of your studies ... you would be an excellent physicist... We are here as the projections today... We are like the light projected in the cinema, though this is a different kind and strength of energy... we are capable of a strengthening or a weakening of the projection, thus we can be even very strong for a few minutes or faded like a mist if necessary... and we are not flat as a two-dimensional picture..

– Mom, but in 1930 when giving birth... you weren't the projection that time(?)... were you?

– No, I wasn't such a projection as I am now, but this is a theme for a different conversation... firmly, not now.

Safona, following her mother's sight, turned her eyes to the lying body. There was Ragna unceremoniously looting the body of all belongings. Only now Safo realised that Ragna hadn't been present in the gymnasium for some quarter of an hour. The body was already stripped of the too-loose-jumpsuit and Ragna was just stripping a dress with a nice floral pattern. Ragna started instructing Safona without eye-contact and continuing the looting.

– Safo, put her dress on!... I am not advising to get dressed in her underwear ... you can survive the journey to West Berlin without knickers... Check her shoes!... is the size good for you?

– They are slightly too big

– They have no heels, so you are not going to harm yourself due to this inconvenience... In West Berlin you need to make some shopping, anyway... In her purse you will find a nice stash of cash...

Now Ragna took a silencer from a jumpsuit's pocket; she attached it to the pistol of GRU-woman and asked ... – Do you know how to use this?

– Yes. This is one of the rare upsides of being the commando's wife.

– I don't think you will have to use this, but.... you know...

... The GRU-woman re-parked your mini before she came to the gymnasium, so it is now in a blind spot; alongside of this building's door... no one from the gate-side nor from elsewhere can see it, thus, you can load her into your car without being seen. I advise you to take a look at your car before you start the loading.

Everybody in "the object" is drunk today.. everybody, to a bigger or lesser extent, nevertheless there are enough weapons and ammunition in your car to pacify them all if something went wrong.

In the car you will find her purse... there is your own legal passport ... Russians obtained it from the Polish passports' office. They obtained also the French, German and Israeli visas for your impostor... all three of them are not entirely legal, but believe me they are very strong... strong enough to reach safely to West Germany... at least. There is also a DDR-transit-visa, but this one is negligible ... I will tell you why, later. The essential things are credit cards and flight-ticket Bonn-Tel Aviv ... it's essential to get rid of this stuff when you arrive in West Berlin. There you have to buy a ticket on the first flight to any city in West Germany or France. Find also the papers hidden under the purse's lining... there are two things... the STASI ID reserved for Russian liaison-officers and the extremely special pass issued by Russian Ministry of Defence... If anybody on the DDR's border will show you any kind of even humble fussiness, just show the ID and treat them like a crap… and don't forget to drop this Russian arsenal somewhere before the DDR's border.

– How could I get out of "the object"?

– You are to drive through its gate… your impostor-girl was supposed to do that, so ….just double the swap.

Safo found a sort of amusement in Ragna's voice.

– Are you sure…?

– I am going to give you a little help… A little should be enough, but … in case if they started grumbling, keep the pistol on the passenger seat ready to use… just kill them if necessary.

– I have never killed anyone… almost never, actually… – Safona turned her eyes onto the body.

– Have you ever used any firearm?

– Quite a lot…

– You will succeed, I know.

– Don't forget "a secret-cubbyhole" which Abel applied to your car… – Aurora joined conversation again. –… you must get rid of its contents too. You can do this in West Berlin when you will find some discrete place for parking your car … somewhere along the wall must be fine … take also number plates… dump all of stuff in some garbage. Then get a taxi and go to the airport…

– I am wondering whether the rest of the GRU-people will be chasing me?

– Not. – Ragna terminated the subject without any hesitations.

– Are you sure? – Ragna only nodded in response. This answer visibly wasn't convincing for Safona, so Aurora took up the topic.

– It is exactly why Ragna is taking part in this operation... She is a sort of specialist. Over the time when you were walking along the beam, Ragna had moved her projection a few dozen kilometres from here and induced an accident... The Mercedes with GRU-people and the frozen couple impacted the van preceding it, carrying the rest of the group on board... as I mentioned before, the Mercedes was specially converted to become a huge torch... it happened, although not exactly on the time, or place where Russians wanted it to happen... though on a railway crossing as it was in the plan... just another railway crossing... There burned out two vehicles instead of one... posthumous examination will show that the victims were drunk.

– Continuing the late-people thread... – It was Ragna's turn for referring. – ...Originally we had planned to leave this discourteous gal in the local commander's bed, which would be confusing enough to deprive the Russians of their will for tracing you, but simultaneously would affect too many branches of the Russian MoD, which would make it harder to sweep this setback under the carpet. She provided us with the alternative idea by packing a trenching spade into your car... When you will be heading to the DDR's border, just stop in some secluded place... there are plenty of such in this area just make a shallow grave and leave her corpse there... we will try to find it and ... and do the proper things.

– What if someone else finds the body before you do... "the proper things"?

– If you will disappear efficiently, then this question will become completely negligible... Perhaps, the Russian will be looking for her alive somewhere in the world but not for a rotten corpse anywhere in Poland...

They will be looking for her alive... this is something which you should be always alerted by, after you reach the West because looking for her they would find you... therefore you cannot use the flight ticket, for instance,... but anyway the carcass is not to give them any hint... even if some Polish authorities found it... This will be just one more unidentified dead Polish girl.

As only the head of the sub-branch of GRU who had approved this operation will realise that you are untraceable, he will start efforts to make the case "the never-existed-one"... He will forget about you, your family and his dead subordinates with inexpressible pleasure...

– You can believe her, my Ferret-pup... Ragna knows them as well as me... And please forgive me...

– Do you want me to forgive you?... The lack of these scientifically-supernatural contacts with me?

– This too... but now I am speaking about something worse ... I mentioned it before ... you have to vanish as if you were dead... it means, not only from the crosshairs of the GRU, but from the lives of your beloved people as well... Please forgive me that I wasn't able to rescue you in a better way... there are some nasty technicalities... a certain range of indeterminacy which is not that bad per se because this is giving some prospect for positive changes too... I am sorry... just forget what I said ... it isn't a solace for you by any means.

One thing is certain, you have to forget about your family to protect them... this is the only thing which matters

– Am I to see you... at least?... You promised to tell me about my birth...

– I will tell you everything you want... And now, you must get to your car ... the key is in the ignition ... count up to 49 and drive... Oh, you must do one more thing...

– What?

– In the corridor ...side of the freezer is a door to the toilet...

– Mom, are you just telling me that I should spend a penny before the journey?

– No, I meant that you should braid your hair... but the pee-idea makes sense too.

Her Charge

Once when Safo had driven out from the blind spot, she got on the drive leading directly to the "object's" gate. She was heading to it very slowly; some 20 kilometres per hour; something curious was happening there; both wardens were out of their booth and giggling with a tall girl who seemed to be drunk; her untidy white blouse was apparently lacking of a few buttons, so her breast was almost exposed.

She had been looking familiar even from afar, but Safo recognised her only when she stopped in front of the barrier; this was Ragna.

They didn't change much in their behaviour as being in front of somebody who should be known for both sentries as a middle-rank GRU officer, thus somebody being several levels higher in the chain of command than they were; apparently they felt fully guarded by the enormous Russian misogyny culture and a bit of alcohol in their veins. None of Russian soldiers would ever dare to show such negligence in front of any male GRU-officer.

One of wardens (still chatting with "the local girl") didn't even turn his eyes on Safona's car; he just pushed the leverage elevating the barrier; the other saluted in a clownish manner as if he was fantasising about himself being the count Andrei Nikolayevich Bolkonsky – he of the Tolstoy's novel.

Safona moved slowly through the gate still hearing Ragna mumbling filthy words in Polish and the Russians giggling in response.

Some 50 meters from the gate was a t-junction where "the object's" drive was joining the public road; Safo stopped the car and pulled the handbrake.

She got a sense of being saturated by a black oily and sticky smog-cloud; it was a mixture of the furious viciousness with the most frantic desire of revenge; of the cruellest punishment for any available Russian.

Just to punish any one Russian for the theft of my life... not the first theft, though perhaps the first that much treacherous.

She saw her own palm on the silenced pistol when she fired directly into the faces of both wardens; she felt the burden of weapon and munitions when she was walking through "the object"; door to door; opening each of them and shooting drunk men who were often asleep; She ran out of munitions for the silenced pistol very quickly, so she heard now the clanging of Kalashnikovs taken from dead wardens, or barking of the Czechoslovakian machine-pistols; she smells gunpowder and blood....

No... this is not going to happen... not today....

Safona released the black cloud, as alike her mini's handbrake and then she took her road.

Some ten minutes later she was passing the town centre navigating towards the DDR's border according to the road atlas. Only one thing interrupted her passage through the town; Suddenly a young woman with a three, or four years old boy appeared in front of her car; it forced Safona to excessive braking. The woman didn't even turn her eyes on Safona's car, whereas the boy was gazing directly at Safona; she got the impression that he was looking into her eyes or even deeper; into her soul; maybe because he so much resembled her own son at the same age; furthermore, he looked like somebody completely unrelated to the young woman leading him through the street.

Safona accelerated slowly still accompanied by the boy's gaze.

Some dozen kilometres from the town, she spotted from afar some irregularity on the road. Getting closer she saw the Polish road-police officers just redirecting traffic.

Is this a trap?

Safona used the time of queuing behind a few vehicles

(mostly lorries) to check discreetly the silenced pistol and covered it with the road atlas on the passenger's front seat. She was determined to fight for her freedom and die for it; she was eternally decided that no one will take her alive anymore.

This was just a normal road-police business on an occasion of a serious traffic accident. After Safona had turned to an alternative road she was able to observe for few minutes as a shunter was just pulling carriages to the nearby station, whilst the proper locomotive was clinched with some burned out vehicles.

Driving over the alternative road Safona spotted a driveway to meadows on a riverbank. She turned into this cobbled road. It was some three quarters on 22.00, so it is not really a dark hour in July.

She stopped the car near the riverbank and re-dressed herself into the jumpsuit. Safona took the trenching spade from her car; cut a 2 meters long piece of turf and pushed it aside; then she removed a bit of soil flinging it over the riverbank. Now, she dropped there the GRU-woman's corpse and most of her deadly belongings onto the body; then she moved the piece of turf back on its place and put onto this a tree branch brought here apparently by the last spring flooding.

Back to the colourful dress, back to the car, back to the journey…

In the frontier town she stopped. The tiredness possessed her almost entirely. Safona took the special papers from behind of the purse's lining and approached the Polish- and then the DDR's border-guard with one of them... the STASI-one... it was much more than enough even for Poles. A potential use of the second paper would be too memorisable and because of that, too much durable in professional gossips. She knew that most men in uniformed- or clandestine services are in fact gossip-mongers.

The distance between the frontier town to West Berlin was approximately 100 kilometres long; not much, but long enough to think too much, especially when her body and mind is just running out of energy.

She was thinking about the fact that the mini with Polish number plates was perhaps the easiest target for shadowing by any surveillance measures.

But what is the alternative?

*If I tried to find other transport I would have to contact some people... each of them could be an agent... if not Russian then STASI... I have very strong papers, but ... but they would appear too strong... My luck is my real pass in most of the probable scenarios, whilst as Abelard used to say "**No one is able to organise the luck**"... fortunately, Russians are not able to organise it for themselves either.*

The recollection of Abel's "proverb" excavated some

deposits of "clandestine logic" involuntarily stored in her memory.

In case of such an operation as this one where they tried to use me and my family I can be 100% sure that nobody knowing anything about it is not going to send an official- or even a semi-official arrest warrant... I cannot rule out, that they have an agent among border-guardsmen, who originally were supposed to support my impostor... this is very unlikely in the case of such a unique operation, but...

But maybe this is even better... After long hours or rather days they will start searching for their female-agent who used the chaos after the traffic-accident to escape with a nice sum of money... If they will interrogate the Polish or DDR's border-guardsmen, they must reach exactly this conclusion, thus they will be looking for somebody with a completely different behavioural pattern... Unfortunately, I cannot rule out that there was a pre-prepared sort of "a silent alert system" related to some ultra-contingency-plan... not "B" not "C" nor even "M" but rather "X" or "Z" ... though this is extremely unlikely... still it cannot be ruled out... In such a case I ... I or, my impostor must be discreetly shadowed before the final engagement ... The good news in such a case is that, such an engagement makes no point until I (or whoever of us two) will reach the West... One of these two is dead... and this fact would be part of the plan "X", but I do not believe that they know which-one, yet... and this is my strength even in such an improbable option...

yet...such plan "X" demands to have a net of not-engaging observers and one who will engage, eventually... will see in the West.

Safona had shown her own passport only to the Berlin-border-police officer entering West Berlin.

This was the time now to abandon her beloved car. Some murky street would be the best for this purpose because the car would quickly find "a new owner" in such a place or at least would be looted to an extent making it unrecognisable; this was a very desirable factor reducing a probability of tracking her route down.

On the other hand however, a walk through such a street was risky in itself and, what was even worse for a deadly tired woman, she wouldn't be expecting any transport means to get out of such a place. She decided to abandon her mini in some reasonable proximity of the first taxi stand she spotted driving along the West Berlin's streets. And she was lucky.

She got a worrisome epiphany when she was just opening the door of a beige Opel car on the taxi stand.

If there is any Russian "engager" then a taxi driver is the perfect profession for such a figure... very well... I am too tired to test the public transport of West Berlin in the middle of the night.

Safona's tiredness deepened; in the simple sentence requesting only a ride to an airport she mixed German with English.

The taxi driver leaned back and answered calmly with the natural Berlin accent:

– OK Mädel[1], but are you wishing the Tegel or Tempelhof-airport … A ride to Schönefeld[2] would be rather complicated.

Safona's answer was too candid, but she wasn't able to control the formulation of her thoughts any longer; she was just happy being able to speak German more-or-less properly.

– I need an airport where I would buy two things as fast as possible … the first thing is a flight ticket to any city in France or West Germany… the second one is … a few pieces of outfit.

– I am not really sure about shops in the airport … I have never bought there anything except pipe tobacco, but I know as a matter of fact that you can obtain the outfit and book the ticket by Kempinski-Hotel… especially if you go there with me … I know everybody there… everyone who we need in such a case, for sure… It isn't even far away from here…

His offer made Safona nervous.

I have never been to Kempinski-Hotel… I know this hotel's name, but everybody knows it… I know even some photos of it… but now it is the night… What, if he is to deliver

---

[1] the lass or the gal
[2] The airport of East Berlin.

me to the Russian consulate?... I did get rid of all my Russian arsenal... I don't have anything to halt him if... Do I have any "weapon-ish"?... car keys?... ridiculous... I have my Polish number plates wrapped in the jumpsuit... he doesn't know what is in... Polish plates are still pressed from heavy steel sheets, what would appear useful once in their history... If he will be stopping in front of a building without the Kempinski-Hotel's sign, I will hit his ear and then open the door, or if he blocked it I will smash the side-window and run calling for police... there must always be police-people in a diplomatic-neighbourhood.

– OK then, bring me to the Kempinski-Hotel... I heard about its many glorious reviews ... let's check them.

– OK then... call me Yorg by the way...

The taxi driver did keep his word. The ticket was booked and the hotel-shop opened just for Safona's shopping.

Yorg refused to take a tip, so she asked him to take care of her mini and to take a 100 Mark note for expenses related to such care.

– ...It should be easy to find a mini without number-plates near the taxi stand where we met... Please take the money... or maybe you need more ...for parking costs(?)...

– I would agree if you give me your autograph on this note

– Autograph?.. but I am not a star by any means ...

– I saw your passport when they were booking your ticket ... Safona... Is this your real name?

– Today... tonight actually I am not really sure of this ... tonight my name is rather Ragna.

– Then you are the star for me ... Please, take my business card... there is my number... Please call me when you will arrive in Berlin-West again... I will tour-guide you through the interesting places which most of tourists will never know about.

– It is not going to happen... soon...

– Doesn't matter, just promise me that you will call

– I promise... it will be my first phone-call... I will call you as soon as I arrive in Berlin ...

...but we both know it is not going to happen ...don't we? ... – Safona completed the sentence in her mind.

She assumed that their encounter's story must drift automatically into an oblivion; that, after some period of time Yorg will sell her mini as a whole or part by part.

Every Polish taxi driver would do that... even the most honourable one.

The first of Safona's tears fell on her seat of the Air France airplane heading Frankfurt am Main. She misinterpreted the cause of the first act of the longest sobbing of her life; she hadn't realised yet, what is really inbound.

She did realise instead what she forgot to say.

In the episode with Yorg, she not only wasn't prudent, nor romantic, but she had left this uniquely good and sensible man with a dangerous "gift". She got some terrible recall when she was some 6000 meters over the planet:

I forgot to get rid of the secret-cubby-hole's contents.

This realisation made her start sobbing as if she hadn't already all those much more serious reasons for crying like the loss of her life and family for ever.

Of course, she had his telephone number, so she would warn him about the dangerous contains of the cubby-hole in her mini, but it would pull an even bigger danger over him.

The cry ceased for a few minutes when she was analysing all the pros and cons of such a call, but then started again and then lasted almost steadily for the next two weeks; and then didn't really stop for over two years.

Suddenly after almost 30 months Safona realised that she was finally able to cease the almost incessant weeping.

It did not happen "just because"... No.

Something had changed within her memories of the 20 July 1969; She was still certain about the weirdness of that day's occurrences, but now it became a considerably different weirdness than it had seemed to be earlier.

20th December 1971

Safona started believing that she had got out of the profoundly dreadful checkmate-situation on her own.

Of course, she hadn't sobbed out her brain over these months, thus she perfectly knew that her escape had had an exactly zero chance to happen without an extremely unique combination of coincidences.

Nevertheless the pictures proving an intervention from outside of our time-space-continuum have faded almost entirely; there was something in her memory, but she has lost sense *What is it*(?) and she wasn't trying to restore such records.

The theory of her "self-sufficiency" accidentally intertwined with the auspicious coincidences was more and more feasible in her eyes... and she actually had good reasons.

She still had in her memory a picture of the two women sitting beside the café-table, but hallucinations are a quite common side-effect of a sedation, especially one which had been done brutally and unprofessionally.

Now, Safo *was almost, almost, almost, almost, almost sure* that after she regained full consciousness, that both women disappeared and had never returned again. She lost even any memories about their identity beside an ambiguous sense of their linkage to her mother.

After the second sedation she woke up completely alone.

She actually didn't notice the button stuck within the locking mechanism before she opened the cage's door by accident; as she woke up naked, she just pushed the door involuntarily during dressing up the jumpsuit left for her by Russians; she spotted the button afterwards.

She spent some time analysing numerous scenarios of potential developments available for her alike for her family. All of them were leading to life-long "special prisoning" or death for herself or for her beloved people, so it doesn't matter which of them was the more consonant with the Russians' goals.

Safona started her reconnaissance along the roof's beam, due to a lack of better options, actually; her instinct was just pushing her to improvise anything.

The GRU-woman entered the gymnasium being visibly upset and already confused about what had made her less watchful. At the very moment Safona was coincidentally hidden behind a big vertical beam; then when the Russian approached the empty cage, she wasn't able to notice where Safona really was, because she was exactly over GRU-woman's head.

Eventually the deadly jump did happen; it just happened.

After almost 30 months Safona wasn't able to detect the sole motive which pushed her to this act and she hasn't seen any reason to find out *What was that*(?) or *Where from it came*(?)

It was just the only logical move amid the anti-logical circumstances.

What would upset the GRU-woman to this extent?

Something extremely serious and utterly unexpected; furthermore it must have been something which cut her off from any pre-arranged sources of guidance.

The very serious traffic-accident was statistically the most probable cause of all these.

A paranoia is usually caused by a deficit of crucial information; this is a universal principle concerning everybody in every type of circumstance.

It is easily imaginable, that an accident happening on a Polish public road was approached by the Polish-traffic police; after the Poles found the Russian military number-plates they had to contact their own regional HQ, which was the only one authorised to contact the nearest command of the Russian military-police which would be 100 kilometres, or more from the collision scene; Safona knew the system thanks to her husband.

She knew from the same source that radio-connections available for such contacts were always faulty; and once again from the same source she knew that nothing is as much a paranoia-making-factor for clandestine-services as unexpected noise around their ultra-clandestine operation.

Why had Safona decided to transport the dead, or nearly dead, GRU-woman out of "the object"?

Perhaps it sounds scarcely believable in our days of 21 century, but in 1969 the fundamental principle of criminology was *No body, means no murder*; and the principle was ruling not only behind the Iron Curtain.

The only available alternative was a staging of a suicide. There however, was at least one big obstacle; it was the other fundamental principle of criminology *No suicide note, means no suicide*; Safona hadn't known the GRU-woman's handwriting; not even to mention that a suicidal person wouldn't drive out of the suicide-scene afterwards; additionally, staging such an act elsewhere wasn't to make any point; a suicide elsewhere wasn't more plausible; a body-smuggling through the gate was risky in both options; burial elsewhere was just the only option.

The GRU-woman re-parked Safona's mini before she came to the gymnasium; she did it for some reason known to her only. Safona discovered this fact, likewise the existence of the blind-spot, when she was making a reconnaissance after her jump and gaining the certainty that the Russian has been "pacified".

She over-cautiously sneaked up into her car and investigated what the Russian left there; Safo started from the woman's purse...

Such an amount of money... big notes of French Francs and German Marks plus a nice bunch of US Dollars... Oh, there is my own legal passport ... Russians apparently obtained it from the Polish passports' office[1]. They obtained also the French, German and Israeli visas for me, or rather for my impostor... all three of them look entirely legal... I had had visas of these three states before and I cannot say whether they are legal or not(?)... perhaps not entirely because I didn't submit any application... anyway they are very strong... strong enough to reach safely to West Germany... at least. There is also a DDR-transit-visa, good for me ... so I can drive my car to West Berlin avoiding airports and railways... There are also credit cards and flight-ticket Bonn-Tel Aviv ... all these latest are useless, or even dangerous... I need to get rid of them... maybe in West Berlin, because in Poland such things would magnetise somebody's attention even on the bottom of a garbage container... I will buy my own ticket... there is so much money that I can buy even a bunch of tickets .... There is something stiff hidden under

---

[1] Over the soviet era, a passport was being given to its owner at the time of travel and was supposed to be returned to the passport office within 2 weeks after arriving back to Poland.

*the purse's lining... Abel always says **that Russians never give up the oldest of spy-tricks**... there are two things hidden... the STASI ID reserved for Russian liaison-officers .... with my name and her photo... her, but somebody tried to make her resemble me... thank you stranger... I am the GRU-captain now ... and the second one hmmm... this is an extremely special pass issued by the Russian Ministry of Defence signed personally by* Андрей Антонович Гречко Министр Обороны[1]*... now only the Kremlin would stop me... and a trenching spade, what for?... There is some huge arsenal on the rear seats... I have to unload this stuff to accommodate her behind the front seats... it is even better... I will use the arsenal to mask her body ... I will bury these things with her ... somewhere before the DDR's border... This arsenal is so huge that it gives me the chance to win even some small battle, so no one will succeed to stop me... no one... not alive... not anymore.*

During the same recon she found a toilet in the corridor. A mirror in the toilet "informed" her that she has to refresh herself and braid her hair.

The only troubles made by Russian soldiers guarding "the object's" gate had an aesthetic nature. Their obscene remarks in Russian language were directed to the female captain of GRU and perhaps only this saved their lives. Safona was wrestling for few minutes with the biggest desire for revenge in her life; finally, she

---

[1] Andrey Antonovich Grechka, the Secretary of Defence (of Soviet Union)

coped with it and drove out of this place.

Safona was thinking about the burial in some woodland, but then the traffic-police re-directed her onto the alternative road passing the riverbank-meadows, so she buried the GRU-woman with her arsenal there.

Unloading her mini in the meadow Safo was wondering:

Why had the Russian clandestine female operator moved my MINI and uploaded it with a trenching spade; 6 Czechoslovakian machine pistols; the same number of pouches with magazines for those pistols and two bandoliers containing hand-grenades? Only heaven might know... Heaven, hmmm... whatever the notion means now.

It didn't even cross Safo's mind that the question which in practical terms was actually already purposeless (during the burial and later) was going to be haunting her for nearly 30 months.

These 30 month-long struggles with the obtrusiveness of a redundant question was in fact something else ... the something else in disguise.

In fact, it was a deadlock between her own qualms of conscience and her confused sense of righteousness, which is actually ironic because this could be disentangled even since day one... If only Safo brought to what her subconscious has known since her first glimpse of the trenching spade... Or if she was able to verbalise, what her instinct had said to her even earlier...

If she verbalised why the instinct had ordered her to jump onto the head of the armed Russian GRU-woman shouting sordid threats in front of the now empty cage.

Apparently Safona's soul had needed this nearly 30 month-long suffering to vocalise the answer.

After such a long agony Safo just found the answer in her mind as if it had never been in a place which could be omitted... as if it had never been playing a hide-and-seek-game with her... as if... whatsoever

O my goodness, she was going to kill and dump me... she was panicking ... their operation had to be more illegal than the entire Russian occupation and its fiasco was lamentable... GRU-woman was going to remove evidences of the operation designed by some highly special cell of GRU; the cell apart from the standard chain of command, because too many elements of the operation went wrong.

Such a setback wasn't supposed to be disclosed even to the eyes of their superior officers let alone to general Ivashutin's, or even worse to the General Staff HQ.

I have no idea what kind of setback had happened... but it was perceived by GRU-woman as a deadly dangerous one and there was no one who would say to her спокойна, продолжай/be calm, keep going... or something similar.

Anyway, she switched to a worse-case-scenario-

procedure apparently on herself... Firmly, this worse-case-scenario had to consist of killing me and ditching my corpse... That is what the trenching spade and grenades were for. My body would become unrecognisable if she detonated a few grenades on my corpse in some pit... even if somebody would find such a grave in the middle of a woodland.

Safona finally vocalised these conclusions to herself and this act eventually really closed one chapter of her life and thereby opened a fresh one.

But before the dawn or the aurora of Safona's new life occurred, however, the entire odyssey had to have happened ... the implausibly lucky jump from the roof's beam... the diversion... the burial of GRU-woman... the arrogant passing of the DDR's border... the acquaintance with Yorg-amazing and romantic Berliner taxi driver ... and the 1000-years-long crying ... It really was like 1000-years-long one though it ceased after merely 30 months... almost 30 ... After nearly 30 months from the moment memorised by entire humankind.

However the humankind did not memorise the moment when the legs of Safona jumping from the beam were just knocking against the body of GRU-woman and crushing her spine... No...

The World memorised this exact moment due something else happening at the exactly the same time... At the very moment somebody else's foot was just making the first human footprint on the surface of the Moon.

Since the day when I have been stripped of my life... since I have been robbed of my life once again... since this day when my life has been taken from me whilst I was left alive... Since that day I achieved plenty of gains potentially structuring my new secure, prosperous and maybe even happy existence, but I wasn't able to succeed in establishing a real new life... I wasn't... until today... For all this time I was believing that I have to defuse the one cruel paradox...

The paradox was consisting of the necessity to forget my own life until 20th of July just to preserve a tiny little fracture of chance for restoring it in an undefined future.... it was necessary because if I tried to restore my old life after the 20th of July events, this would almost certainly end as a fiasco annihilating any chance for some restoration later.... on the other hand, pretending that I am able to continue the same life after losing access to everyone or everything I loved was the certified road to severe mental disorder....

Back in my old life I was so many times translating texts where numerous authors were trying to describe indescribable paradoxes... so many times I was questioning in my mind a plausibility of their attempts... so many times I was mocking the absurdity of their narratives' twists... And finally I had found myself in such a story being condemned to get out from this on my own...

Not that many times, but still many... I was translating professional texts ... and despite the fact I was supported by professionals, I had had to learn a lot of their knowledge to avoid e.g. a misleading structuring of some key-sentence... I knew for instance that the human's memory isn't a scientifically objective recording of occurrences, emotions or ordeals... functionally the entire library of our memories is not much more than a story based on true events.... I was so knowledgeable and so stupid by the same means... I was looking for grand turning points instead of pivotal details... It is to be changed, now.

Afterword

The Novella you have just read is not a solitary piece of writing; it is a small part of a substantial series.

A long time ago I got the idea of writing a novel exploring one of my greatest fascinations – i.e. a paradoxical symbiosis of vulnerability and durability.

Over the course of decades, I have been studying and contemplating the paradoxical and mysterious bond between both these notions intertwined within the souls and minds of individuals facing overwhelming historical-, political-, or social factors.

On a certain stage of my studies, I have realised that their bond is not as paradoxical as it seems to be, because both those notions are, in fact, rooted in the same features or the same blue-print of a given individual; and as intertwined they put the power of altering reality in the hands of the powerless individual.

After years of considerations I realised that to conclude my observation I must turn them to a written form; that in order to convey the power of the bond between seemingly contradictory notions I need to engage a human's psychology without obsessive psychoanalysis; to engage a mystery without a mysticism; a supernaturality without a horror; history without submissiveness to ideology; science without a gadget-mania; and fiction without inventing stories or protagonists, but rather discreetly deriving them from out of our world's variety.

But, who is to read such a trans-disciplinary writing produced by someone without a degree in social science (at least)? So, I needed to write my observation as embedded into a fiction. But, still, this was too complex to be delivered within a single novel, thus, to present and systematise my observations there were needed a series of novels. But, what kind of novels?

Hence, I came to the conclusion, that I must invent a new genre; or rather re-invent and revitalise in a contemporary manner something existing in 18th century as a **_Bildungsroman_** or in 19th century's Romanticism as the digressive poems or novels (e.g. **_The Anhelli_** by Juliusz Słowacki).

The most essential difference is that I am aiming to create an independent novel-system and therefore it must consist of at least 11 parts.

Eventually over the period 2013– 2014 I wrote the first novel of my series (_Yuriy and Abel: The Himmerland_

Manoeuvre) and the second one (*An Eleventh Shore*) one year later.

Preparing the third part (*In the Name of Orsha*) I started by writing a short story as a form of sketch/draft for the third novel. Finally, the short-story turned out to be rather a novella by its size.

The short-story/novella[1] (*Mistress Cartographer of the Un-Light*) belongs to the at-least-eleven-parts-long novel-series, either in the form of an independent novella or as the first chapter of the complete novel (*In the Name of Orsha*).

Seemingly the series is a one family's saga commenced from the WW2 time (with some references to a more distant past), and in fact the entire series tells the story of Safona, her husband Abel, and their children; the story embraced in several alternative ways; story of people of flesh and blood having their real archetypes in real history, not two-dimensional human-screens used to project some ideas on them.

Nevertheless, there is one additional protagonist whose ubiquitous presence in a variety of manifestations turn an ordinary family-saga into something else; into the modern version of **the Bildungsroman.**

---

[1] The original version had been written as the short-story/ a sketch for the third novel, but at some stage of the translation process I realised that it is much too sketchy, thus some sections have been expanded. The short-story turned to be the novella.

The crucial part of my novel-system is also a multiple repetition in repainting this family portrait in several alternative versions; in the several alternative time-space-continuums; illuminated through several prisms; however, avoiding repetition of the same episode because this would be boring for the reader.

For instance, the first novel (*Yuriy and Abel: The Himmerland Manoeuvre*) brings and bundles the numerous real historical threads related to Safona's family, leading to a fictional global episode of 1983, whereas the second novel (*An Eleventh Shore*) tells about occurrences of the 1990s and 2000s based on reality amended by a single alternatively unfolded episode of 1959.

One might ask, why I am not trying to publish the first novel; the one which acquaints the reader with the cartography of the entire series, as the novel is a so-instructive-compass for my independent genre(?)

The answer is rather trivial: originally, all these three texts hadn't been written in English. I have just completed the translation of the short-story/novella, and only this one is available in English as yet.

The novella (*Mistress Cartographer of the Un-Light*) brings a relatively humble portion of answers to the conundrum of the phenomenon between vulnerability and durability, but it reflects the method of my genre very much in a tangible way.

I hope that the release of the first book will pave the way for publishing the entire series in English, i.e. two already existing novels which must be translated; the third which will contain the novella as its first chapter; and no-less than eight additional volumes, which exist currently only in the form of basic drafts.

The progress of writing, translating and publishing needs an acceleration, but it is extremely difficult to achieve this by working alone. Therefore, I am inviting anyone (not only professionals) to support this acceleration.

Anyone who would support the translating, or publishing processes in any form, please contact me at my email address: **ro.cherry@hotmail.co.uk**